PHARMACEUTICAL INDUSTRY DOCUMENTS

90 Pharmaceutical Quality Assurance Interview

Questions & Answers

BY

CHANDRASEKHAR PANDA

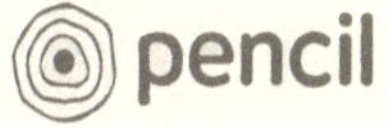

ISBN 978-93-5438-939-9

Published in India 2020 by Pencil

A brand of
One Point Six Technologies Pvt. Ltd.
123, Building J2, Shram Seva Premises,
Wadala Truck Terminal, Wadala (E)
Mumbai 400037, Maharashtra, INDIA
E connect@thepencilapp.com
W www.thepencilapp.com

AUTHOR BIOGRAPHY

The author of Pharmaceutical Industry Documents is Chandrasekhar panda who is having more than 13 years of Experience in Pharmaceutical Quality Assurance department and he has worked in various Pharma companies like Cipla, USV & Aurobindo Pharma Limited.

The author is also having a Pharmaceutical Blog named pharmaceuticalupdates.com and written various articles or topics regarding Pharmaceutical industry.

CONTENTS

90 Pharmaceutical Quality Assurance Interview Questions & Answers

1. What is Quality Assurance:

Quality Assurance is a deep concept covering all matters that individually or collectively influence the quality of a product. It is the complete & whole of the arrangements made with the object of ensuring that the manufactured products are of the quality required for their intended use.

2. Responsibility of Quality Assurance:

In process checks during manufacturing & packing activities, Providing Line clearance in Manufacturing, Packaging and Warehouse, Sampling of products in manufacturing and packing, Reviewing the manufacturing and packing batch record, Issuance of documents to other departments, calibration of Instruments, Providing training to other department, Ensuring online documentation and compliance throughout the plant,Review & approve Standard operating procedure, change controls and deviations.

3. What is tablet ?

Tablets is defined as the solid unit dosage form of medicines with suitable Excipients and prepared either by molding or by compression. It comprises a mixture of active substances and Excipients, usually in powder form, pressed or compacted from a powder into a solid dose.

4. Name any three tablet processing problems :

Mottling, Capping, lamination, picking and sticking

Mottling- unequal colour distribution of a tablet.

Capping- Partial or complete separation of a tablet top or bottom crowns.

Lamination- Separation of tablets into two or more layers.

picking- Because of adhesion to the punch faces, Localized portion missing on the surface of the tablet.

Sticking- Adhesion of tablet localized portion to the punch faces resulting in rough and dull appearance.

5. What is Disintegration Test :

It is the time required for the Tablet / Capsule to break into particles, the disintegration test is a measure of the time required under a given set of conditions (Temperature) for a group of tablets/capsules to disintegrate into particles.

Cycle of shaft holding the tube basket limit is 29-32 cycles per minutes and distance covered by shaft basket is 50-60 mm and beaker temperature is 35 to 39 º C.

Disintegration is to be performed to determine whether tablets or capsules disintegrate within the prescribed time when placed in a liquid medium at the experimental conditions.

6. What are the Disintegration Time of tablets :

Uncoated Tablet 15 min as per BP & 30 min as per USP

Sugar Coated Tablet 60 min as per BP

Film Coated Tablet 30 min as per BP

Plain Coated Tablets DT in specific medium for 30 min as per USP

Enteric Coated Tablets DT in simulated gastric fluid (0.1 M HCl) for 1 hr and then in simulated intestinal fluid (Phosphate buffer 6.8 pH) until disintegrates as per USP.

Dispersible Tablets 3 min (15- 25º C) as per BP.

Effervescent Tablets 1 tablet in 200 mL water for 5 min (15- 25º C)

as per BP

Buccal Tablets 4 hrs as per USP.

Soluble Tablets 3 min (15- 25º C) as per BP.

Chewable Tablets are not require to comply with test

7. What is Disintegration Time of capsules :

Gastro resistant capsule DT 2 hrs without disk in 0.1 M HCl and phosphate buffer pH 6.8 for further 60 min as per BP.

Hard and Soft gelatin capsule DT 30 min as per BP & USP.

8. What is Friability Test of Tablet & friability Calculation:

Friability is defined as the percentage of weight loss of powder from the surface of the tablets due to mechanical action and the test is performed to measure the weight loss during transportation.

Friability (%) =W1– W2/W1X100

Where,

W1 = Weight of Tablets (Initial / Before Tumbling) &

W2 = Weight of Tablets (After Tumbling or friability)

Limit : Friability (%) = Not More Than 1.0 %

Tablets with individual weight equal to or less than 650 mg then take the sample of whole corresponding to as near as 6.5 gram equivalent and tablets with individual weight more than 650 mg then take sample of 10 whole tablets to perform friability test. Tablets must be de-dusted prior to and after use.

9. Weight Variation limit for Tablets and Uniformity of Mass Variation:

Weight variation Limit for Tablets& Uniformity of weights Variation

Average weight in mg		Percentage deviation %	Uniformity of weight variation as per IP, BP and Ph Eur.	
IP/BP	USP			
80 mg or less	130 mg or less	± 10 %	Average Weight in mg	Percent-age devi-ation %

More than 80 mg or less than 250 mg	130 mg to 324 mg	± 7.5 %	Less than 300 mg	10 %
250 mg or more	More than 324 mg	± 5 %	300 or more	7.5 %

10. What is Validation:

Documented program or evidence, that provides a high degree of assurance that a specific process method or system consistently produce a result indicating predetermined accepted criteria.

11. What isValidation Protocol :

A written plan starting how validation will be conducted and identifying specific acceptance criteria. For example the protocol for a typical manufacturing process identifies processing equipment's, critical process parameters/ operating ranges, Critical Quality attributes and product characteristics. Sampling and test data to be collected, number of validation runs and acceptable test results.

12. Prospective Validation:

Establishing documented evidence that a system does what it supposed to do prior to the commercial distribution of the new product or an existing product made by a new or modified process.

13. Retrospective Validation:

Establishing documented evidence that a system does what it purports to do based on a review and analysis of historic information. It is normally conducted on the drug material already being commercially distributed and is based on accumulated production, testing and control data.

14. What is Calibration?

The demonstration that a particular instrument or device produces results within specified limits by comparison with those produced by a traceable standard over an appropriate range of measurements.

15. What is Qualification?

The action of proving that any equipment or process work correctly and consistently and produces the expected result. Qualification is part of, but not limited to a validation process, i.e. Installation Qualification (IQ), Operation Qualification(OQ) and Performance Qualification (PQ).

The act of planning, carrying out and recording the results of tests on equipment to confirm its capabilities and to demonstrate that it will perform consistently as intended use and against predefined specification.

16. What is User Requirement Specification :

A requirement specification that describes what the equipment or the system is supposed to do, thus containing at least a set of criteria or condition that have to meet.

Detailed design & functional specifications shall be taken from the supplier for a particular piece of equipment / instrument / system / facility. The same shall be prepared by User &reviewed by Engineering & Quality Assurance. Based on the specifications, URS document shall be prepared

17. What is Factory Acceptance Test?

A Factory Acceptance Test is usually preformed at the vendor prior to shipping to a client. The vendor tests the system in accordance with the clients approved test plans and specifications to show that system is at a point to be installed and tested on site.

18. What is Site Acceptance Test?

A Site Acceptance Test the system is tested in accordance to client approved test plans and specifications to show the system is installed properly and interfaces with other systems and peripherals in its working environment.

19. Design Qualification:

Documented verification that equipment, instrument, facility and system are of suitable design against the URS and all key aspects of design meet user requirements.

20. Installation Qualification (IQ) :

The documented verification that all components of the equipment and associated utilities are properly installed or modified in accordance with the approved design and manufacturer's recommendations.

21. Operational Qualification:

Operational qualification consists of verification and documentation, of the parameters of the subjected equipment. The documented verification that the equipment, instrument, facility and system as installed or modified, perform as intended throughout the installed operating range.

22. Performance Qualification:

Performance Qualification is designed to prove the process, can consistently produce a product that meets the stated requirements and specifications. It is a documented verification that the equipment, instrument, facility and system as connected together, can perform effectively and reproducibly, based on the approved process method and product specification.

23. Why Three consecutive batches taken for Validation:

Consecutive meaning following closely with no gap or following one after another without interruption.

The number of batches to be taken under validation depends upon the risk involved in the manufacturing Critical process parameters & critical Quality Attribute so depends upon that manufacturer have to choose the number of batches to be validated.

If we will consider less than two batches then the data will not be sufficient for evaluation of and to prove reproducibility of data between batch to batch variation & if we consider more than three batches it can increase the time & cost of manufacturer which usually not preferred.

Generally if we will require quality in the First batch, then it is accidental (co-incidental), Second batch quality is regular & third batch quality is Validation or Confirmation.

Statistical evaluation cannot be done by considering two points, because two points always draw a straight line so minimum three points required for comparison of data.

24. In An Oral solid dosage Manufacturing Facility 'positive' Pressure is Maintained In Processing Area or Service Corridors :

In tablet manufacturing facilities, pressure gradients are maintained to avoid cross contamination of products through air. Usually processing areas are maintained under positive pressure with respect to service corridors.

25. What is Positive Pressure :

Atmospheric pressure which is higher than the immediate surrounding areas usually measured in inches of water or Pascal.

26. What is Cross Contamination :

Contamination of a material or product with another material or product is called cross contamination.

27. What is Schedule -M :

Good manufacturing practice and requirements of the Premises of the plant, Waste disposal and equipment's.

GMP has two parts Part I and Part II

Part I is GMP for Factory Premises and Part II is GMP for Plant & equipment's.

28. What is Quarantine in pharmaceuticals:

The status of the materials isolated physically or by other effective means, pending for a decision on their subsequent use. Materials are kept in Quarantine area with proper status labeling.

29. What is Relative Humidity:

It is the ratio between the actual amount of water vapor present in certain volume of air at a given temperature and the maximum amount of water vapor that the air can retain at that temperature.

30. Expiry/Expiration Date:

The date usually placed on the containers /labels of material designating the time during which the material is expected to remain within the established self life specifications if stored under defined conditions and after which it should not be used.

31. What is Deviation?

Any unwanted event that represents a departure from approved processes or procedures or instruction or specification or established standard or from what is required. Deviations can occur during manufacturing, packing, sampling and testing of drug products.

Examples of Deviations: Temperature and RH of area goes out of limit during manufacturing, Typographical error observed in approved documents, Standard operating procedure not followed, Breakdown of equipment, Spillage of material during unloading, Instrument calibration results goes out of limit etc. Deviations are of three types Minor, Major and Critical.

32. When to take Deviation:

Deviation has to raise for the following criteria mentioned below (But not limited to)

- Temperature and RH of area goes out of limit during manufacturing
- Typographical error observed in approved documents
- Standard operating procedure (SOP) not followed
- Breakdown of equipment & Spillage of material during unloading, loading etc.
- Instrument calibration results goes out of limit

33. What is Minor, Major and Critical deviation:

Critical deviation: A Critical Deviation is an unplanned event that affects a quality attributes a critical process parameter, an equipment or instrument critical for process control and has an immediate patient safety risk, life threatening situations.

Major deviation : A Major Deviation is an unplanned event that potentially affects a product's quality, safety or efficacy or its ability to meet specification, or regulatory or documentation requirements which may not have direct impact on patient.

Minor deviation: A Minor deviation is an unplanned event that potentially has GMP impact (e.g. an event affecting a utility, equipment, materials, components environment or documentation) but does not affect product quality and / or the physical state of the product, intermediate or component, or it's labeling.

34. Who is Observer and Initiator in deviation :

The person identifying the occurrence of deviation shall be termed as observer and the person initiating the documentation of deviation in deviation form shall be termed as Initiator.

35.When deviation shall be raised :

Deviation shall be notified to the concern department and QA for review, evaluation and logging within one working day after occurrence.

36. For which type of deviation Risk Assessment is required:

Quality risk assessment shall be performed for suspected product defects, potential impact on other batches or on other products etc. Wherever applicable

37. For deviation investigation report which type of tools shall be used :

The tools like Ishikawa diagram analysis (fish bone diagram), 5 why's, fault tree analysis (FTA) failure mode and effects analysis (FMEA), Flow charts, Process flow etc. shall also be used for detection of the root cause, if necessary.

38. What to do if actual root cause is not identified during investigation :

If actual root cause is not identified, potential root cause shall be identified based on history of repetitive deviation, deviation trends, vendor assessment, scientific knowledge and actions shall be taken to prevent the potential from occurring.

39. What is the frequency of trending of deviation :

Periodic review of deviation system or Trending of deviation shall be conducted quarterly to check the effectiveness of deviation system and shall be documented.

40. What will be the contains of periodic review or trending of deviation :

Periodic review shall include (but not limited to) total no. of deviations during review period as per category (e.g. Critical, Major and minor), as per department, as per nature of deviation (e.g. Product related, Process related, equipment related, calibration validation failure, testing related etc.), no of repeat deviations (e.g. as per nature and as per root cause etc), department wise classification of deviation, Category wise, Type wise, Review of similar root cause, Review of previous open, Summary and conclusion.

41. When CAPA to be initiated from deviation :

Depending on the impact assessment / risk assessment, identified root cause, and comment received from various sources, Corrective action and preventive action (CAPAs) shall be defined by responsible department head in consultation with QA.

Appropriate CAPA's shall be identified and subsequently logged into CAPA log book and the deviation report shall be closed.

QA shall check the implementation and completion of the corrective and preventive action and update the Log book.

42. Are all the deviations shall be forwarded to customer or Qualified person and CQA for Approval:

Yes All products related deviations (critical, major, and minor) having impact on product quality, safety, and efficacy, validated status of process & equipment shall be circulated to the customer/Qualified Person/Marketing Authorization Holder for notification and approval.

All the deviations shall be sent to CQA for approval

43. What is the timeline for closing of deviation :

All deviations shall be timely reviewed to close within 30 calendar days of occurrence of deviation & Justification for delay in closure shall be filled by the responsible department in case deviation is not closed in 30 days.

Only two extensions, of 30 days each, shall be allowed for Investigation & deviation closure, if failed to complete the activities after two extensions, then Quality Risk Assessment shall be prepared by responsible department.

44. Who shall be included in investigation team of deviation:

The cross functional investigation team shall be formed for the investigation of deviations and shall consist of Head of the department or designee where deviation has occurred and members with sufficient knowledge on current matter for investigation.

The team shall include members (depend upon nature and Applicability) from QA, QC, Manufacturing, Packaging, Regulatory, Engineering, Safety and Warehouse etc.

45. Who will perform investigation for deviation :

The responsible department head/designee shall initiate the investigation as per the SOP for Investigations as applicable, considering history & trending, root cause evaluation, risk and impact assessment and comments from other departments within the site along with QA department.

46. What is Change Control:

It is an Approved Procedure which is taken to change in any documents, Standard operating procedures, Specification, Process parameters and change in batch size etc. Change control is raised by user department as per requirement and finally the change control is approved by Quality assurance.

Change control can be raised through software or through manually.

After Final approval of change control the changes can be made in documents and change control can be closed after completion of required action plan which is mentioned in the Change control form.

Change controls are of two types' i.e.Major and Minor.

47. When to take Change Control:

Change control has to take for the following criteria mentioned below (But not limited to)

1.

1. Change in Manufacturing process
2. Change in Product formulation
3. Change in HVAC systems / Air handling systems / air filtration systems;
4. Change in Batch / lot size
5. Change in Manufacturing, packaging and analytical equipment;
6. Change in Facilities & Utilities & Water systems
7. Change in Raw Materials, Intermediates, Packaging materials
8. Change in Analytical testing methods & specification,
9. Change in Manufacturing Site

10. Change in Stability (shelf life, retest period, storage and transport conditions)
11. Change in Pharmacopoeia or existing monograph
12. Artwork related changes
13. Addition, deletion of new equipment or new product.
14. Changes in Batch documents (Batch Manufacturing Record and Batch Packing Record)
15. Changes in Standard Operating Procedure (SOP)Changes in Calibration schedule and Preventive Maintenance for all instruments

48. Who shall fill the change control form & who will review the same

The initiator shall fill the required details in change control form with Current status, proposed change, appropriate reason or justification for change, Assessment of the change and the risk analysis and department Head of initiator department shall review the change control form along with all supportive data and supportive information.

49. What is the responsibility of change control coordinator

The change control coordinator shall review the change control form filled by the initiator & enclosed documents for correctness & completeness.

The change control coordinator shall also review the risk assessment provided for the change, if acceptable shall proceed for next stage.

The change control coordinator shall select the reviewer departments for impact assessment and comments and based on the details provided, change control coordinator shall categorize the change control as major and minor.

50. For which type of Change Control Risk Assessment Report is required

Quality risk assessment report shall be prepared during change evaluation. E.g. New product introduction at site, Addition of alternate source of API, Addition of alternate source of Empty Hard gelatine capsule, change in Batch size, (i.e. addition of higher capacity equipment's) and introduction of new equipment's at site etc.

51. What is Major Change in Change Control

Any change in the product, production process, quality controls, equipment, facilities, or responsible personnel that have a substantial potential to have an adverse effect on the identity, strength, quality, purity, or potency of the product as they may relate to the safety or effectiveness of the product.

E.g. Addition/ / deletion of New API source or change in existing API source, Introduction of New Product at site and Change in Manufacturing Formula/ Manufacturing Process/ Batch Size, Installation/Modification of Critical Equipment like Fluid Bed Equipment, Rapid Mixer Granulator, Change in packing process and change in specification for Raw and packing materials.

52. What is Minor Change in Change Control

Any Changes in the product, production process, quality controls, equipment, facilities, or responsible personnel that have a minimal potential to have an adverse effect on the identity, strength, quality, purity, or potency of the product as they may relate to the safety or effectiveness.

E.g. Change in format or document and change in Standard Operating procedure and editorial changes, Modification/ Elaboration of Standard Operating Procedures, Revision of RM/PM analytical method for Correction of typographical error etc.

53. Are all the change control shall be forwarded to Regulatory affairs for comments

No all change Control shall not be forwarded to Regulatory affairs for comments but submission or filling batches related Change controls, validation related change controls etc. shall be forwarded to RA to know the regulatory impacts as per US and Europe variation requirements.

54. Which type of change control shall be forwarded to Customer or Qualified person for comments or Approval or notification

All the product related change control (change in batch size, addition of alternate sources of Active pharmaceutical Ingredients or Empty hard gelatin capsule, Change in product shelf life, and change in packing material etc.) Shall be forwarded to the customers or Qualified person for Approval or notification

55. What is the timeline for Closing of Change Control

All change control forms shall be closed within 90 days from the final approval or as per target completion dates and two extension (90 days for each) can be taken for closing of change control with justification for delay but Change control closing timelines shall not be applicable for change controls raised for the introduction of new product at site.

56. What happen if change controls are not closed within timeline

If the change control are not closed within the specified timeline after extension Quality risk assessment report shall be prepared to justify the risk of not implementing the changes

57. What is the frequency of review and trending of change control and what will be the contains of change control trend

Change control shall be reviewed on monthly basis to know the status of open change controls and Trending of the Change control shall be done on Quarterly basis.

The review shall comprise minimum of the no. change controls initiated, approved, closed, overdue during the review period. The change control review may be carried out department wise, category wise, type wise and any specific highlights during the review period like repetitive temporary change controls.

The effectiveness of the changes implemented during review period shall be included into the review.

Change controls e.g. equipment related, facility related, system related change controls which are implemented and closed can be considered for the verification/review of the effectiveness of implementation.

58. What is the Responsibility of Head QA in Change contro

All the change controls shall be approved by Head Quality assurance after compilation of actions required for implementation and shall be responsible for the seeking approval from Marketing authorization holder, Customer, CQA, Qualified person (QP).

Head QA shall review the change control log monthly for status of change controls and completeness and correctness of change control log and take necessary actions for any overdue change controls.

59. What is Like to Like Changes in change control

Replacement of a piece of equipment by another one with identical characteristics and function (same material of construction, size, type etc. but not necessarily from the same manufacturer).

These changes might have very minor effect or no effect on critical parameters, critical attributes or equipments functionality, however impact of these changes shall be accessed through site procedure for preventive maintenance and breakdown maintenance (e.g. Replacement of minor identical parts during breakdown or preventive maintenance)

60. How change control shall be closed

Upon completion of all the activities stated in action plan of change control, initiator shall send the duly filled change control form along with all attachments (i.e. supporting documents) to QA for review and closure.

The change control coordinator shall review the change control form along with all supporting documents for completeness and correctness and ensure that all necessary actions are completed.

Upon satisfactory review of QA, Change control form shall be closed and same shall be updated in change control log.

61. Corrective action:

An action taken to eliminate the cause of the existing deviation, incident or problem in order to prevent its recurrence (occurring again).

Corrective Action shall be taken after the event.

62. Preventive action:

An action taken to eliminate the cause of potential deviation, incident or problem in order to prevent its occurrence (an incident or event).

Stop the incident from happening (before event)

CAPA is taken to rectify the problem or incident or deviation or event etc.

63. CAPA can be routed from which activities :

Corrective Action and Preventive Action can be routed or generated from the following activities (But not Limited To)

a. Deviation

b. Customer and Regulatory Audits at the site

c. Critical equipment / instrument breakdown

d. Customer/ Regulatory complaints or Market Complaints

e. Product recalls and Repeated failures of the systems

f. Vendor audits

g. Self Inspection at site (whether Internal or Corporate Quality Assurance)

h. Rejections of the material (Raw materials, Packing materials and Finished Product)

i. Annual Product Quality Reviews

j. Out of Specification, Out of Trend, Incidents

k. Mock exercises e.g. recall, safety mock drill, etc

<u>64. When CAPA shall be closed:</u>

Authorized persons from QA shall monitor the CAPA for its completion.

On Completion of required actions the department head (imparted department) shall certify that proposed CAPA is completed and implemented.

QA shall verify the implementation and completion of CAPA by review of supporting documents and certify the same.

Based upon the CAPA the required changes done shall be shared to the user and other impacting department and required training shall be imparted.

65. How CAPA Effectiveness shall be checked:

CAPA effectiveness shall be done with Trend review of various CAPAs derived from incidents or events.

CAPA effectiveness checks include the review of the repetitive CAPAs & the same shall be considered satisfactory if no repetitive CAPA is observed.

CAPA effectiveness check can also be verified from the review system like Annual Product Quality Review, surprise checks, spot checks and during internal audit.

66. What is Hold Time Study?

Hold Time studies establish the time limits for holding the materials at different stages of production to ensure that the quality of the product does not degrade significantly during the hold time at a required temperature and Relative Humidity.

67. What is Site Master File?

A Site Master File (SMF) is a document that describes the structure of the organization which includes the site, the manufacturing activities carried out, the facility and premises, number of employee with their Qualification, Production system, Quality Control System and also details of the quality management system which are in place.

It contains General information about the plant, Quality System, Personnel, Premises and Equipment's, Production system, Documentation, Quality Control system, Self Inspection and site inspection history etc.

68. What is VMP:

A Validation Master Plan is a document that summarizes the firm's/organizations overall philosophy, intentions and approach to be used for establishing performance adequacy. It provides information on the firms/organizations validation work programme and defines details of and timescales for the validation work to be performed, including a statement of the responsibilities of those implementing the plan.

It contains the validation policy, Process & Cleaning validation, Qualification & Requalification, Computer validation, Utility validation & Qualification, Vendor Qualification, Temperature mapping, Change control, Deviation, Risk Assessment, Standard Operating procedure, Training, Area Qualification, calibration and Preventive maintenance & closure of VMP etc. VMP shall be updated yearly.

69. What is Control Sample :

An appropriately identified sample that is representative of each batch that shall be retained is known as control sample. These are also referred as retention or reference sample.

The control sample shall be collected at the initial, middle and at the end of packing operation of the batch and the details of the total pooled quantity collected shall be entered in the respective Batch Packing Records with sign, date & sample collection time.

70. How much sample to be collected for Control or Reference Sample:

The control sample should consist of twice the quantity required for complete analysis and Sample quantity shall be decided on the basis of specifications given by Quality Control.

Control sample shall be collected for Raw material, Packing Material and Finished Products.

71. What are the tools used for Investigation in Pharmaceuticals:

The tools are Brain Storming,Fish Bone diagram, 5 Why, Affinity Diagram or Chart, Root cause analysis, Failure Mode Effect Analysis etc.

72. What is Cleaning Validation :

It is documented evidence which provides us the assurance that a cleaning procedure is consistently removing product residue from equipment.

Three batches shall be taken for Cleaning validation After the Cleaning procedure for the equipment's are validated, periodic monitoring / Cleaning verification shall be done once in year on worst case product.

73. What is Worst case in cleaning validation :

The product selected from a group of products that represents a greater risk of carry over the residue of previous product to next product manufactured using the same equipment by virtue of its solubility, Cleanability, Permitted daily dosage exposure, toxicity or a combination of these factors, therapeutic dose, etc.

It is the case or condition where there is a chances of Product failure.

74. What is Line clearance:

Line clearance is a process which provides a high degree of confidence or assurance that the said line or area is free from any unwanted residue or left over of previous processing's before proceeding for next process. Quality assurance has to provide Line clearance before the start of any activity whether it is batch to batch change over and Product to product change over.

Line clearance shall be given by Quality Assurance at Raw material Dispensing stage, manufacturing stage, Packing stage and in Quality Control before start of any activity.

75. Water Validation Phases:

Water system validation has been categorized into 3 phases: Phase I, Phase II and Phase III.

Phase I Requires a 2 – 4 weeks (14 days minimum) testing period in order to monitor the system deeply.

Phase II is continuity of previous phase i-e phase I, it carries the sampling plan same as previous phase plan & it also facilitates the monitoring of system for 2 – 4 weeks (30 days) period.

In phase III sampling locations and frequency reduced as compared to previous phases. Phase III represents that the water system shows reliable under control attainment over such a long time period & Phase III typically runs for one year after the satisfactory completion of phase II.

76. What is Concurrent Validation:

Concurrent validation is used to establish documented evidence that a facility and process will perform as they are intended, based on information generated during actual use of the process.

77. What is Product Recall & Mock Recall:

A product recall is a request from a manufacturer to return or removal of a marketed product after the discovery of safety issues or product defects that might endanger the consumer or put the maker/seller/ manufacturer at risk of legal action.

Mock means Make a Duplicate or exact copy of something.

Mock recalls are routine exercises conducted by manufacturers, processors, distributors and other various trading partners in the supply chain to assess or verify their recall procedures and responsiveness and to train the recall team.

78. What are the in processes checks parameters during Tablet compression:

Appearance, Group weight, Individual weight variation, Uniformity of weight, Thickness, Diameter, Hardness, friability, Speed of machine, compaction force, die fill depth and Disintegration time.

79. What are the In processes checks parameters during Capsule Filling:

Appearance, Group weight of filled capsule, Individual weight of filled capsule, Net fill content of the powder, locking length and Disintegration time.

80. What are the In processes checks parameters during Tablet coating:

Appearance, Inlet temperature, out let temperature, pan RPM, Gun distance from tablet bed, spray rate, weight gain, Group weight of Coated tablets, Individual weight of Coated tablets, and Thickness.

81. What are the challenges at capsule filling in case validation batch:

Speed of the Machine (low and high speed), Hopper study (half-filled hopper and one fourth filled hopper), Start, Middle & end of capsule filling at optimum parameters, Composite sample for complete analysis and Dissolution profiling. The sample shall be collected in duplicate.

82. What are the challenges at tablet compression in case validation batch :

Speed of the Machine (low and high speed), Hopper Study (The machine is equipped with powder level sensor, collect the tablets once before the powder is about to go below the sensor) Sample shall be collected at Start, middle and End of the compression to perform Uniformity of dosage unit by content uniformity and other physical parameters as per batch record, Tablet Hardness (low and High Hardness) to perform physical parameters and Dissolution profiling on tablets and Composite samples at optimum parameters.

83. What are the samples collected at blending stage in case Validation:

At Pre-lubrication and Lubrication stage samples shall be collected equivalent to 1X-3X doses from 11 different locations in triplicate to perform Blend Uniformity and after lubrication Blend composite sample shall be collected Assay, LOD or Water by KF, Untapped Bulk Density and Tapped Bulk Density and Sieve analysis.

84. What is Definition of Product Recall:

Removal or correction of marketed products for the reasons relating to deficiencies in quality, safety or efficacy, including labeling considered to be in violation of the laws.

Wholesale Level: All distribution levels between the manufacturer and retailer.

Class I Recall: Notification and acknowledgement of receipt of recall notification within 24hrs.

Class II Recalls: Notification and acknowledgement of receipt of recall notification within 48 hours.

Class III Recalls: Notification and acknowledgement of receipt of recall notification within 5 days.

Mock recall shall be done to evaluate the effectiveness of arrangements periodically to recall the products from EU / US / Australia / other export markets and domestic markets. Mock recall is applicable only to markets where product is already marketed.

Frequency of Mock Recall shall be once in two years or as per MA Holder / Contract giver requirement.

85. What are the possible reasons for the Non-conformities

The following are the possible reasons, but not limited:

- Management attitude
- Ineffective documentation
- Lack of trained personnel
- Lack of co-ordination / co-operation within or among departments.

86. What is HACCP

HACCP : Hazard Analysis Critical Control Point

87. What are specifications of Purified water as per any pharmacopoeia

A. Tests	Ph. Eur.
Description	Clear, colorless liquid
Acidity /Alkalinity	The solution is not colored red/The solution is not colored blue.

Oxidisable substances	The solution remains faintly pink
Chlorides	The solution shows no change in appearance for at least 15 min
Sulphates	The solution shows no change in appearance for at least 1 hour
Ammonium	Maximum 0.2 ppm.
Calcium and magnesium	A pure blue colour is produced.
Residue on evaporation	Maximum 0.001 per cent
Aluminum	Maximum 10 ppb,
Nitrates	NMT 0.2 ppm
Heavy Metals	NMT 0.1 ppm
Conductivity (At 25°C)	NMT 5.1ms.cm-1
Total viable aerobic count	NMT100 CFU /ml
Pathogens : E. coli Salmonella Pseudomonas Staphalococcus aureus	Absent Absent Absent Absent

88. Briefly explain about ICH climatic zones for stability testing & long term storage conditions

ICH STABILITY ZONES Zone Type of Climate

Zone I Temperate zone

Zone II Mediterranean/subtropical zone

Zone III Hot dry zone

Zone IVa Hot humid/tropical zone

Zone IVb ASEAN testing conditions hot/higher humidity.

89. What needs to be checked during AHU validation

During AHU validation, following tests shall be carried out

- Filter efficiency test,
- Air velocity & number of air changes,
- Air flow pattern (visualization)
- Differential pressure, temperature and RH
- Static condition area qualification
- Dynamic condition qualification
- Non-viable count · Microbial monitoring
- Area recovery and power failure study.

90. What is a significant change in stability testing

1. A 5% change in assay for initial value.
2. Any degradation products exceeds its acceptance criterion.
3. Failure to meet acceptance criterion for appearance, physical attributes and functionality test.
4. Failure to meet acceptance criteria for dissolution for 12 units.

www.ingramcontent.com/pod-product-compliance
Lightning Source LLC
LaVergne TN
LVHW050428160726
843469LV00041B/1273

* 9 7 8 9 3 5 4 3 8 9 3 9 9 *